MW00912474

DONATED BY

**THE WOMAN'S CLUB OF
ROYERSFORD**

For my children who inspired the story, my husband who gave me unwavering support, and my family and friends who gave me honest feedback and lots of encouragement.

www.mascotbooks.com

Giving Hope: A Child's Journey Through a Pandemic

For more information, please contact:
Mascot Books
620 Herndon Parkway, Suite 320
Herndon, VA 20170
info@mascotbooks.com

Library of Congress Control Number: 2020919577

CPSIA Code: PRT1220A

ISBN-13: 978-1-64543-755-0

Printed in the United States

GIVING HOPE

A Child's Journey Through a Pandemic

Written by
Toni Wengerd, Ed.D.

Illustrated by
Andrew Littlefield

March 5, 2020

This was a busy week. Every day we had something to do after school: dance class, gymnastics, scouts, horseback riding, soccer, and even viola lessons. It's been hard to get my homework done!

Overwhelmed

March 10, 2020

Today my mom asked what type of birthday party I would want this year. I think maybe I'll ask for a horseback riding party. Ever since I did a pony ride on vacation, I have loved horses. I just started taking riding lessons and it is the best! A horseback riding party would be super fun!

Excited

March 12, 2020

Today was just a normal day, but then the phone rang. My mom looked worried. Then she said school was going to be closed for a few weeks because a lot of people were getting sick with a new virus. I hope we don't get sick.

Worried

March 18, 2020

So much has already changed, and it's only been a few days. All of our activities are being cancelled. Maybe this is why I needed to have this journal.

Disappointed

March 23, 2020

My dad started working from a computer set up in my bedroom. He comes down for snacks and lunch. It's strange that he's not at work. Sometimes I like sharing my room with him, but sometimes I wish I had it all to myself again.

Uncertain

March 24, 2020

Our days are so different. My mom makes us do our
  schoolwork instead of our teacher, and she always makes us
play outside, even in the rain. We've done projects, played
  games, planted seeds, and we always draw with chalk in
  our driveway.

Confused

March 30, 2020

Today I asked why we are still staying home so much. We are always home. We never drive anywhere. My mom and dad said school will probably be closed for the rest of the school year.

Sad

April 1, 2020

I miss my friends and family. I am sad about all of the activities that are being cancelled. I asked my mom when we could go back to school and when we could see our family and friends again. She said not for a while, but then she said that there are some things we could do that might help. Things that could give hope while times are so hard. How can we give hope when nothing seems to be going right?

Frustrated

April 2, 2020

Hope? What does she mean? What is hope anyway?

Curious

April 3, 2020

Today we wrote letters—actual letters. We wrote to our grandparents, aunts, uncles, cousins, friends, and even people we don't know. They were simple letters telling them we care. Will that give someone hope?

Wondering

April 4, 2020

Today we got to "see" our grandparents on the computer. We got to talk to them, show them things, laugh, and smile. It almost felt normal. Will seeing people on the computer give hope? Tomorrow we get to see our teachers on the computer and my sister will have a virtual dance class. On Sunday we'll get to have church on the computer. It's different. I just want to be with my friends again, but I guess this is okay for now.

Content

April 8, 2020

I heard about something called "essential workers." They are people who have to go to work even though we have to stay at home. People like doctors, nurses, the mailman, grocery store workers, delivery truck drivers, and many more. These people are so brave to keep going to work even though they could get sick. I wonder how we can thank them and give them hope, too.

Inspired

April 15, 2020

This afternoon we met a few families at a nursing home where there are a lot of really sick people. My mom said even the people who work there are sick. I was a little nervous because we all had to wear a mask. I don't like the masks. I didn't understand why we were there or how we could help.

Anxious

Then, my mom took out some chalk and we all started drawing pictures and writing words of hope on their sidewalk. We told them they were heroes and that it was going to be okay. We drew hearts, flowers, and rainbows. While we were drawing, I saw other people dropping snacks and cards off at the front door. I guess other people are doing things to give hope, too.

Honored

April 17, 2020

We loved the chalk messages of hope so much that we
started to decorate our sidewalk at home with words of
hope for our neighbors to see as they go on walks.

Encouraged

April 23, 2020

Today is my birthday! I turned ten. I can't have a party or see my family and friends to celebrate, but they all made an amazing birthday video! They sang, played instruments, did funny skits, and talked to me. I loved it! Then, my neighbors did a drive by birthday parade...for me! They honked horns and dropped off posters and cards they had made for me. It wasn't a horseback riding party, but I still felt pretty special.

Excited

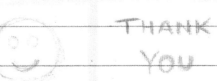

April 29, 2020

On Sunday, we heard that our church is doing a Give Hope Project. They are collecting lots of different things to give to people in need. We decorated some boxes and told the neighbors what we were collecting. We put the boxes in our driveway for people to drop off items for us to bring to church. Some neighbors asked what we were doing and said they'd be back to donate. After two days, we had lots of bags filled with food and supplies!

Grateful

May 5, 2020

Today was supposed to be the art show at our school. Since it was cancelled, my neighborhood decided to do a neighborhood art walk. The kids put artwork out at the end of their driveway for the neighbors to see. My whole family went for a long walk to look at all of the artwork. Even my art teacher came! He drove around honking and telling us how proud he was. This really made me feel that everything is going to be okay. Maybe not today, or tomorrow, but someday it will be okay.

Confident

May 8, 2020

I've been hearing about other ways people are trying to bring hope to the community. We've seen people putting candle lights in their front windows at night and delivering meals to hospitals. I heard about people offering free concerts. There are virtual book readings and outdoor story walks. There are so many ways that people are trying to inspire others.

Thankful

May 14, 2020

When this is all over and I get to see my friends and family again, I'm going to ask them some important questions.

What gives you hope during difficult times? Is it something you did? Is it something someone did for you? Then, I'll remind them that no matter what we are faced with, there are always ways to give hope.

Hopeful

Dear Reader,

This story was written during the COVID-19 pandemic. However, there are many other challenging things that people go through. In fact, maybe your COVID-19 experience was much more difficult than the one in this story. During challenging times, I encourage you to think about ways to give hope. It might make a very difficult situation a little easier to get through. One thing you can try is journal writing or drawing. Use the emotions below to write or draw about what you are going through. Maybe writing or drawing about your experiences and emotions can be a way to give yourself, and others, hope.

~Blessed

Emotions List:

Overwhelmed   Excited   Worried   Disappointed
Uncertain   Confused   Sad   Frustrated   Curious
Wondering   Content   Inspired   Anxious   Honored
Encouraged   Grateful   Confident   Thankful
Scared   Nervous   Happy   Tired   Hopeful   Blessed

Dr. Toni Wengerd is a wife, mother of four, and an elementary school teacher. She has been a public school educator in Pennsylvania for nineteen years. Her free time is dedicated to her family, and she can be found volunteering with the children's ministry at her church. Her children were the inspiration for this story as they navigated the shutdown during COVID-19. This is her first children's book, but she's hoping to publish another heartwarming story in the future.

 Though this is his first time illustrating a book, Andrew Littlefield has loved drawing since he could hold a pencil. By day he works as an application developer and designer. He's also a husband, father, and multi-instrumental musician. He enjoys volunteering with any activity in which his two sons are involved.